C O N N E C T I

MW01181201

California, Here I Come!

MARILYN S. ROSENTHAL
DANIEL B. FREEMAN

Series Editor: John Rosenthal

Boston   Burr Ridge, IL   Dubuque, IA   Madison, WI
New York   San Francisco   St. Louis
Bangkok   Bogotá   Caracas   Lisbon   London   Madrid   Mexico City
Milan   New Delhi   Seoul   Singapore   Sydney   Taipei   Toronto

McGraw-Hill

*A Division of The **McGraw·Hill** Companies*

Connections Readers: California, Here I Come!

This book is printed on acid-free paper.

domestic 1 2 3 4 5 6 7 8 9 0 DOC DOC 9 0 0 9 8 7
international 1 2 3 4 5 6 7 8 9 0 DOC DOC 9 0 0 9 8 7

ISBN 0-07-292778-X

Editorial director: Thalia Dorwick
Publisher: Tim Stookesberry
Development editor: Pamela Tiberia
Production supervisor: Tanya Nigh
Print materials consultant: Marilyn Rosenthal
Project manager: Shannon McIntyre, Function Thru Form, Inc.
Design and Electronic Production: Function Thru Form, Inc.
Typeface: Goudy
Printer and Binder: R.R. Donnelley and Sons

Grateful acknowledgment is made for use of the following:
Still photography: Jeffrey Dunn, Ron Gordon, Judy Mason, Margaret Storm

Library of Congress Catalog Card Number: 97-75582

http://www.mhhe.com

Job Hunting

At Nancy's house

Nancy's renters, Melaku and Angela, welcome Rebecca.
So do Nancy and Uncle Edward.

Melaku cooks Ethiopian food. They all eat together.

1

Rebecca calls her brother Kevin. She asks about her father.

Nancy is crying. She's sad. Edward is sick. He can't come to the house again.

2

Melaku leaves his rent check on the table.

Rebecca talks to Nancy about the rent.

3

At the San Francisco College of Music

SAN FRANCISCO   COLLEGE OF MUSIC

① *I'm sorry. We don't have a job for you now. There's no money.*

② *No job? What am I going to do?*

③ *Look on the bulletin board.*

Rebecca goes to the college. She asks María Gómez about her job.

Rebecca looks on the bulletin board. There are no jobs.

A Bad Day

In downtown San Francisco

Rebecca buys a newspaper. She looks for a job in the newspaper. She calls about the jobs.

Rebecca has a job interview. The job is not right for her. She doesn't get the job.

Rebecca goes to her next interview. The man sits too close to her. He touches her shoulder. She doesn't want the job.

At Nancy's house

Rebecca tells Angela about her day. Angela understands.

Alberto calls Rebecca. He's going to show her San Francisco. Then he's going to take her to a restaurant.

7

A Night Out

The sights of San Francisco

Alberto shows Rebecca the Palace of Fine Arts.

Rebecca sings for Alberto.

It's a beautiful song.

My mother wrote it.

There's San Francisco.

It looks far away.

Alberto and Rebecca are walking together. They are happy.

At the Casa Mendoza restaurant

Alberto takes Rebecca to Casa Mendoza. It's his family's restaurant. Rebecca meets Alberto's mother and father.

Alberto and Rebecca are eating Mexican food. They're talking and having a good time.

Alberto's mother and father are talking about Rebecca. They like her.

Rebecca meets Alberto's brother. His name is Ramón. He works in the restaurant with his mother and father.

Ramón tells Rebecca about a job. It's at his son's school.

Alberto takes Rebecca home.

First Day of Class

At the San Francisco College of Music

Professor Thomas is teaching a music class at the San Francisco College of Music. The class is very hard. Rebecca and Bill Ellis are students in the class.

At the after-school program

Rebecca has an interview with Emma Washington at Alex Mendoza's school. There is a job in the after-school program.

Rebecca meets Alex Mendoza and his best friend, Vincent Wang.

Rebecca plays baseball with the students. She helps Vincent.

Mr. Wang comes to the school. He takes Vincent home.

At the restaurant

At the restaurant, Mrs. Mendoza talks to Ramón.

Alberto talks to Ramón, too.

Casey at the Bat

At the after-school program

Rebecca takes the job at the after-school program. Now she's teaching baseball. The children like her very much.

Rebecca, you're doing a great job.

Emma Washington is happy. Rebecca is a good teacher.

At Nancy's house

Rebecca gets flowers from Alberto.

The next day, Rebecca looks at the flowers again. She thinks about Alberto.

Rebecca calls her father. He is sick, but he doesn't tell Rebecca.

At the San Francisco College of Music

Professor Thomas is teaching his class. The students are playing guitars.

At the after-school program

Emma Washington is talking to Ramón.

Ramón and Alex talk about guitar lessons. Ramón sees Rebecca. She doesn't see him. She's meeting Alberto.

The Art Gallery

Alex and Ramón are eating ice cream. Alex asks Ramón about his divorce.

At the restaurant

Ramón gets a letter. It's from Christine. Christine is Alex's mother.

At the gallery

Alberto takes Rebecca to a gallery. There are many people. They are looking at the photographs.

Alberto shows Rebecca his photographs. There's a photograph of Alex and Ramón.

Alberto and Rebecca see many people. They are all looking at one photograph. It's a photograph of Rebecca. She can't believe it. Alberto named the photograph "Dream Catcher."

Thank you, Alberto. I had a wonderful time.

Alberto takes Rebecca home. He gives her a present. It's a dream catcher. They kiss goodnight.

At the restaurant

The Mendoza family is talking about the restaurant.

Ramón and Alberto are talking. Alberto gives Ramón a letter. It's for Rebecca.

The Picnic

The children are having a party. Ramón is there.
Vincent's mother and father are there.

The children are playing games. They are having a good
time.

24

Ramón and Rebecca are talking. Ramón gives Rebecca
Alberto's letter. It's about a party for Mr. and Mrs. Mendoza.
Ramón and Rebecca are becoming friends. Rebecca is going
to go to the party.

Two boys come to the party. They are not in the after-school program. They fight with Vincent and call him bad names. Alex helps Vincent.

The children in the after-school program watch the fight. They are laughing at Vincent. They are laughing at the bad names.

Rebecca helps Vincent. Ramón is very angry.

Mr. Wang is very angry, too. He takes Vincent home.

27

Prejudice

At the after-school program

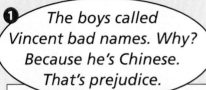

1 *The boys called Vincent bad names. Why? Because he's Chinese. That's prejudice.*

2 *But many of you laughed at Vincent. That's prejudice, too. That wasn't right.*

Emma and Rebecca are talking to the children about Vincent. Officer Jones comes to the class. She talks about prejudice. The children understand now. They feel bad. They are sorry.

At Vincent's house

Vincent is talking to his mother about the after-school program.

At the after-school program

The children miss Vincent. They all write letters and cards to him.

Alex reads his card to Rebecca.

A Difficult Decision

Emma and Rebecca go to Mr. Wang's store. They give the cards and letters to him.

Emma understands prejudice, too. She tells Mr. Wang about her life.

At the Wangs' house

Mr. Wang gives the cards to Vincent. Vincent likes the cards. He misses his friends.

At the after-school program

Mrs. Wang is talking to Emma Washington. Vincent is not coming back to the program.

Rebecca tells Alex about Vincent.

Ramón meets Alex at school. Alex tells Ramón about Vincent. Then he tells him about the guitar lessons.

Guitar Lessons

At the Wangs' house

Rebecca is talking to Mrs. Wang and Vincent about guitar lessons.

Mrs. Wang thanks Rebecca for the lessons. She gives Rebecca a present. It's a Chinese vase.

At the Mendozas' house

Ramón and Alex are talking about Rebecca.

Later, Ramón and his mother talk about Christine.

Mrs. Mendoza helps Alex with his homework. They talk about Ramón and Christine. Then they talk about Ramón and Rebecca.

At the after-school program

Ramón tells Rebecca about Christine. Rebecca is Ramón's friend. She listens to his problems.

The Retirement Party

At the Mendozas' house

Alex is very angry. He wants his mother. But he also wants his father.

Alex goes to his room. He doesn't understand. Ramón talks to him and helps him.

Ramón hugs his son.

At the retirement party

There's a mariachi band. They're playing Mexican music. Mr. and Mrs. Mendoza are dancing. People are singing and having a good time.

Alberto takes Rebecca to the party. Rebecca says hello to the Mendozas. She meets Mrs. Mendoza's friend, Alice Goodman.

Rebecca talks to Ramón at the party.

Alice Goodman and Carmen Mendoza are talking about Rebecca.

The Phone Call

At the retirement party

Alex is sad. He's thinking about Los Angeles. Rebecca gives Alex a four-leaf clover key ring.

Ramón and Alex made a beautiful cake for Mr. and Mrs. Mendoza. It's a wonderful party.

My wife and I worked for 30 years. Now we're retiring. But Casa Mendoza is not going to close. We're not selling the restaurant. The Mendoza family is keeping Casa Mendoza.

Here's to the next 30 years.

The Mendozas thank their sons and their friends.

Carmen Mendoza is
dancing with Alex.

Alberto is dancing with
his friend, Gloria.

Ramón is dancing with Rebecca.

Nancy Shaw and Angela come to the party. There's a
serious problem. Kevin called. Rebecca's father is in the
hospital.

Rebecca calls Kevin. She's going to Boston tonight.